W9-CPY-208

An Adams' Wood Mystery

WHO STOLE THE PRIZE?

Follow the clues and find the answer

Written by Stewart Cowley
Illustrated by Susi Adams

DERRYDALE BOOKS
NEW YORK

Published 1986 by Derrydale Books,
distributed by Crown Publishers, Inc.

Produced for Derrydale Books by
Victoria House Publishing Ltd.
4/5 Lower Borough Walls
Bath BA1 1QR, England

Copyright © 1986 Victoria House
Publishing Ltd

All rights reserved. No part of this
publication may be reproduced, stored
in a retrieval system, or transmitted,
in any form or by any means, electronic,
mechanical, photocopying, recording or
otherwise without the prior permission
of the copyright holder.

Printed in Belgium

"Hello, I'm Holmes Mouse, the great detective!"

"And I'm Watson Mouse, his best friend!"

This is a story about our friends who live in the woods, and their Sports Day. What a day it was! Somebody stole the big trophy cup. Will you help us find it?

Read the story and look at the pictures carefully to find the clues. We will be looking for clues, too—watch out for us.

If you don't solve the mystery we've put together all the evidence in one big picture near the end of the book . . . and if you still don't know who stole the prize, we may have found the answer for you.

It was Sports Day in Adams' Wood and everyone had
come to watch. The sun was shining, and even though
it was early in the morning it was already quite hot.
"Let's get started!" cried Mr. Raccoon, the referee.

"Oh dear," said Mr. Rabbit. "Are we starting already?" He had been marking out the racetrack with a brush dipped in white paint, and he hadn't quite finished!

Mr. Rabbit painted the last line just as the sack race was beginning. How funny Sammy looked as he wobbled his way to the front. He was sure to win. He'd been practicing for weeks!

Robbie was trying to win the pole vault contest. He ran toward the bar, vaulted high into the air—and yes, he was over! Scrambling to his feet, he jumped for joy and dashed off to tell his mother.

Longtail came in first in the long distance running race.
"Well done, Longtail," said Benjy Bunny.
"Phew!" gasped Longtail. "I'm so hot!"
"You should have a drink," said Benjy.

"Quick, Mrs. Rabbit! Longtail needs a drink!"

Mrs. Rabbit shook her head. "You can't have any lemonade yet, Longtail," she said. "The glasses haven't arrived. I'll go and find them."

Mr. Squirrel was organizing the egg and spoon race.
"Hold your spoons steady," he told the runners.
"Don't let your eggs fall off!"

When the races were over, it was time to award the
prizes. Mr. Fox was going to hand them out. "Are all
the winners here?" he asked.

"Wait!" said Mrs. Fox. "Someone is missing.
Where is the winner of the long distance running race?
He should be here to collect the big cup!"

Suddenly there was a shriek from Miss Mouse at the prize table. "The big cup is gone!" she cried in a panic.

Mrs. Hedgehog ran over to see what was happening
and slipped on some wet grass. "That's funny," she
said. "It hasn't rained for days . . . and this puddle
smells of lemons!"

"There's no time to worry about lemons!" exclaimed Mr. Frog. "We must find the cup. Longtail will be so disappointed if he misses his big prize."

"Oh no! Mr. Frog has missed a clue!"

Reddy the Robin spotted something on the ground. "It's only someone's race number," he said. "That's not going to help us find the cup."

"But that race number must belong to somebody . . . ."

"Here's the winner's rosette beside the
race number!" shouted Mr. Beaver.
"Come on, everyone—I have an idea
who has the cup . . . haven't you?"

"Have you guessed?
Turn the page and see
who's hiding."

"That's better!" sighed Longtail happily, as he drank
the last drop of lemonade from the big cup. "Oh, sorry
everyone! Were you looking for me?"